P9-BYN-004

Echo's
Lucky Charm

Dolphin School

Echo's Lucky Charm

by Catherine Hapka
illustrated by Hollie Hibbert

SCHOLASTIC INC.

If you purchased this book without a cover, you should be aware that this book is stolen property. It was reported as "unsold and destroyed" to the publisher, and neither the author nor the publisher has received any payment for this "stripped book."

No part of this publication may be reproduced or stored in a retrieval system, or transmitted in any form or by any means, electronic, mechanical, photocopying, recording, or otherwise, without written permission of the publisher. For information regarding permission, write to Scholastic Inc., Attention: Permissions Department, 557 Broadway, New York, NY 10012.

ISBN 978-0-545-75025-7

Text copyright © 2015 by Catherine Hapka
Illustrations copyright © 2015 by Scholastic Inc.

All rights reserved. Published by Scholastic Inc.
SCHOLASTIC and associated logos are trademarks and/or registered trademarks of Scholastic Inc.

12 11 10 9 8 7 6 5 4 3 2 1   15 16 17 18 19 20/0

Printed in the U.S.A.   40
First printing, March 2015
Book design by Jennifer Rinaldi Windau

1

Bay's Announcement

"Hurry up, Pearl—we don't want to be late to Magic class!"

"I'm coming!" Pearl called to her friend Echo. "Wait for me!"

She waited one more moment as a large grouper swam in front of her. Coral Cove Dolphin School was located in a quiet lagoon sheltered by a large, circular coral reef. Lots of sea creatures lived on or near the reef, so there were always plenty of fish, mollusks, and crustaceans swimming or crawling through the school.

As soon as the grouper had passed, Pearl flicked her tail to catch up with Echo. Just ahead, their friends Splash and Flip were waiting for them.

"We'd better hurry," Splash said, doing a somersault in the water. "Bay doesn't like it when we're late."

Pearl smiled. She knew they weren't going to be late. But it was no surprise that Splash wanted to swim faster. He loved swimming fast, doing flips, jumping, and spinning.

"Okay, let's go!" Pearl said. "I hope we practice our guiding today. It's so much fun!"

One of Pearl's favorite parts about going to school was learning all about dolphin magic. As the protectors of the ocean, dolphins used their magical powers to help other creatures. For instance, Pearl's family pod lived near an island where sea turtles hatched. Her parents helped the baby turtles swim safely out to sea and find food, mostly by using a magical ability known as guiding. That was a type of mental magic in which dolphins sent gentle messages to other creatures to show them what to do. Pearl couldn't wait to get better at magic so she could help her parents help the baby turtles!

Soon Pearl and her friends were swimming into the part of the cove where they went for Magic class. The rest of their school pod was already there. On the first day of school, the teachers had divided all the students into smaller groups for their classes. There were eight dolphins in Pearl's school pod, including her and her three best friends.

"It's good to see you all again," Bay said. Bay was Pearl's favorite teacher, and she taught Pearl's two favorite subjects—Magic and Music. The pod had already had Music class that day.

"Is everyone ready to get started?" Bay asked.

"I'm ready!" Splash exclaimed, doing a flip.

"Good. I have an important announcement today," Bay said. "You've all been doing very well in class, so I've decided you're ready for your first test. It will be three days from now."

A test? Pearl blew a nervous stream of bubbles out of her blowhole. This would be their very first test since starting school just a few days earlier. Pearl wasn't sure she was ready!

"Now let's get to work so you're prepared for the test," Bay said. "We'll start today by practicing our guiding. Be patient for a moment—I need to call over some creatures to help us."

She began to sing. A small school of about

a dozen brightly colored cardinal fish swam closer, attracted by Bay's beautiful song.

Bay stopped singing and looked at the class. "I want you to divide into pairs and try guiding these fish," she said.

Splash's eyes widened. "All of them at once?"

Pearl felt nervous again. Her parents often guided whole groups of baby turtles. But so far, Pearl and the other students had only tried their guiding skills on one creature at a time.

Well, most of the other students . . .

"Have you done this before?" Pearl whispered to Echo.

Echo's mother had especially strong magic. She was famous all throughout the Salty Sea because she'd once saved a whole group of Land Leggers from drowning when their boat sank. Even though most young dolphins waited until they started school to learn any magic, Echo's mom had already taught her a little bit.

Echo nodded. "Mom helped me guide a small school of angelfish a few times," she whispered back. "By the way, do you want to be partners?"

"Of course!" Pearl said.

The other two female dolphins in the pod went first. Bay told them to try guiding the cardinal fish into turning around and swimming the other way. Pearl could see that the girls were trying hard. But they only got one of the cardinal fish to turn the way they wanted. The others got confused and scattered in every direction.

"Oops," said one of the girls, a slender little

dolphin named Harmony. "I hope that's not on the test."

Bay chuckled. She sang a few notes of her song to bring the school of cardinal fish together again. "Don't worry. I know this is a more difficult exercise than anything we've done so far," she said. "Pearl, Echo—why don't you give it a try?"

"Okay," Pearl said. She and Echo swam to the surface to take a breath of air. When they were back underwater, the two of them touched their fins together. Magic was always stronger when dolphins worked as a team.

"Ready?" Echo asked. "Let's guide!"

Closing her eyes, Pearl focused her magic energy, adding it to the energy already pouring out of Echo. When she opened her eyes, Pearl saw that the fish had all stopped. They were hanging still in the water, fins vibrating.

"More!" Echo whispered. Pearl saw her friend touch the pretty striped shell she always wore as a necklace. Even more energy pulsed out through the water.

"Hey!" Splash exclaimed. "There they go!"

The fish were moving again—this time in the opposite direction! Pearl sent out one more burst of energy, feeling proud of herself and Echo. They'd done it!

"Good work, girls!" Bay sounded pleased. "Very good."

Magic was the last class of the day. When Bay dismissed the class, Splash and Flip stayed behind to talk to the other boys in the pod. Pearl and Echo swam slowly toward the school entrance.

"We were great partners, weren't we?" Echo

said to Pearl. "We were the only ones who got all the fish to turn around at the same time!"

"Yes, that was fun." Pearl smiled. "I saw you touch your shell while we were doing it. How come?"

Echo touched her necklace again. "It's my lucky shell," she said. "My mom gave it to me."

"Oh, right. You told me that before." Pearl nodded. "But why do you call it your lucky shell?"

"Because I think it must have a little bit of my mom's magic in it," Echo explained. "I always do better at magic when I touch it."

"Really? Cool!" Pearl looked at the necklace again, impressed. She wished she had a lucky shell of her own!

2

Echo's Idea

PEARL AND ECHO HAD JUST LEFT THE SCHOOL reef when Splash and Flip caught up to them. "Wow, can you believe we're having a test already?" Splash said, doing a flip beside the girls. "I hope I pass it!"

"I definitely will," Flip said. "I bet I'll get the best score of anyone on that test!"

Pearl just smiled. When she'd first met Flip, she'd thought he bragged too much. But now she was starting to get used to it—plus, he was bragging less than he had been.

"I hope we're all ready," she said. "Do you think we'll have to guide more than one creature at once, like we practiced today?"

"Maybe," Echo said. "The test isn't for three whole days. Bay might think we should be able to learn to do that by then."

Splash looked nervous. "Uh-oh. Flip and I couldn't get any of the fish to turn!"

"That's because you got distracted and did a flip while we were trying," Flip complained. "I could feel that they were about to turn!"

"Hey, Flip, I have an idea," Echo said. "Pearl and Splash should come home to our pod with us so we can all study together."

Echo and Flip were part of the same pod. A pod was a dolphin family, although not all dolphins in a pod had to be related. Some pods were small and the dolphins who lived in them were always the same, like Pearl's—she lived with only her mother, father, and younger sister. Most pods were larger, with dolphins joining or leaving all the time. For instance, Echo and Flip's pod had more than fifty dolphins in it! Pearl had never been around such a large pod before. She was nervous to visit—but excited, too!

"That's a great idea," Splash said. "Let me find my brother and tell him. He can let the rest of my pod know where I am. Be right back!" He swam off in a flurry of bubbles.

Pearl didn't have any older brothers or sisters at school. "I'll have to go home first so my parents know where I'm going," she told Echo and Flip. "I don't think I can send them a mental message from this far away."

"No problem," Flip said. "We'll come, too."

As soon as Splash returned, the four friends set off. They swam quickly through the shallow, warm waters of the Salty Sea. Pearl lived farther from school than any of the others. But the trip seemed shorter with her friends along. Before she knew it, they were swimming between two large coral formations into a quiet lagoon.

"Wow, it's pretty here!" Echo said.

"It's too bad no turtle eggs are hatching right now," Pearl told her friends. "You'd love the baby turtles—they're so cute!"

A younger dolphin zipped toward them. "Hi, Pearlie!" she said. "Hey, who are you guys? Are you Pearlie's friends?"

"This is my little sister, Squeak," Pearl told the others. "Squeak, these are my friends Echo, Flip, and Splash."

Squeak looked impressed. Like Pearl, she'd grown up in their small pod, far away from most other dolphins. She immediately started asking the others all sorts of questions. Meanwhile, Pearl swam off to find her parents and get permission to visit Echo and Flip's pod.

Then Pearl and her friends said good-bye to Squeak and set off. They found Echo and Flip's pod in the shallow, sun-flecked water between two large islands. There were dolphins of all ages everywhere Pearl looked—eating, talking, or just swimming around. Pearl hung back behind the others, feeling shy. Several younger dolphins around Squeak's age were playing in the surf near one of the islands under the watchful gaze of several adults. One of them, a large female with big eyes, spotted

Echo and the others and swam over.

"Hi, Mom." Echo rubbed fins with her mother. "Pearl and Splash came over so we could all study together. I hope that's all right."

"Of course. Welcome, young ones." Echo's mother smiled. Suddenly colorful lights flickered all around Pearl and her friends, bursting in pretty shapes that reminded Pearl of lace coral, and ending with a beautiful underwater rainbow that rippled in the current.

"Wow!" Splash exclaimed. "Did you do that?"

"Sure she did." Flip shrugged. "She's awesome at magic, remember?"

Echo's mother chuckled. "That's just my way of saying welcome," she told Pearl and Splash kindly. "I'm glad you're here. Echo never stops talking about you two!"

"Really?" Pearl felt shy. She'd heard so much about Echo's mother and her super-strong magic. And seeing that amazing light display, she could believe it! All adult dolphins could create pretty displays like that out of light and water droplets. But Pearl had never seen one as bright and interesting as the one Echo's mother had just made.

"What are you kids studying today?" Echo's mother asked.

"Magic," Flip replied. "Bay's giving us a test

in a few days. I'm not that worried about it, but these guys are." He swirled his fin toward the others.

Echo's mother chuckled. "Bay is a good teacher. She'll make certain you're well prepared. But it can't hurt to practice together, either."

"Will you help us study?" Echo asked her mother.

"I'll be around if you need me," her mother replied. "But I'm sure you're all smart and talented enough to do well on your own."

Just then, one of the baby dolphins squeaked for help, and Echo's mother swam off to check on him. "I'm glad your mom will help us study if we need her," Splash said. "It's too bad she can't come to school to help us out with the test, too!"

"Yes." Pearl glanced at Echo's necklace, once again wishing she had one of her own. "But at least Echo always has a little bit of her mom's special magic with her in her lucky shell."

Echo touched her shell and smiled. "Come on," she said. "Let's practice some magic!"

3

An Unexpected Visitor

PEARL LOVED MUSIC CLASS ALMOST AS MUCH as she loved Magic class. The next day, her school pod worked on singing together. It wasn't easy—some of the dolphins sang faster or slower than the others. And Splash tended to get distracted and start doing flips in the middle of the song.

"Oops," he said when he did that for the third time. "Sorry about that, you guys."

"It's all right, Splash," Bay said. "It's time to end class, anyway. We'll continue working on this tomorrow, since singing together can help make our magic stronger. See you in Magic later. Class dismissed."

Pearl touched Splash's fin with her own. "Don't worry," she told him. "I can tell you're getting better at singing."

"Thanks, Pearl." Splash smiled gratefully. "Come on—let's go to Jumping and Swimming. I'm much better at that class!"

Pearl's smile faded. Splash might be good at Jumping and Swimming, but not Pearl. She still wasn't used to swimming fast or jumping much at all. She didn't have to do any of that stuff in her quiet, safe lagoon!

As she followed the rest of the pod out of the music area, there was a sudden loud whistle from the middle of the cove. It was Riptide, the Jumping and Swimming teacher. He was floating beside Old Salty, the head of the school.

"Attention, all students," Old Salty said, using magic to make his voice loud enough to be heard in every nook and cranny of the reef. "I have an important announcement. An electric ray just swam into the cove."

"That's right," Riptide boomed out. He was a large, burly dolphin with a brisk manner. "As you know, rays don't normally bother dolphins."

Old Salty chuckled. "Most of them know that," he told Riptide. "But not the first years. We haven't covered rays in Ocean Lore class yet."

"That's true," Echo whispered to Pearl with a giggle. "I think Old Salty got stuck on mollusks and algae!"

Pearl giggled, too. Old Salty taught their Ocean Lore class. He seemed to know everything there was to know about every creature, plant, and type of coral in the Salty Sea, but his lectures were kind of boring.

"In any case," Old Salty continued now,

"we want to make sure our electric ray friend has moved on before we continue classes. We wouldn't want anyone to get a shock! So we'll have recess early today. Please stay in the area near the kelp forest until we tell you it's safe."

When Pearl and her friends reached the kelp forest, most of the older students were already there.

"I wonder how long it will take the teachers to move the ray," Splash said, using his tail to play with a swaying frond of kelp.

"Probably not long," Echo guessed. "Bay is great at guiding. I'm sure she'll be able to convince the ray to leave."

That reminded Pearl about the Magic test. "Speaking of guiding, who wants to practice with me? We could try to guide those oysters over there to open and close their shells."

"During recess?" Flip said, sounding surprised.

Pearl nodded. "I really want to be ready for that Magic test. It's only two days away now, and I'm getting nervous!"

Three older students swam over just in time to hear her. One was Splash's older brother, Finny. The other two were Finny's friends Mullet and Shelly.

"Uh-oh," Mullet said with a smirk. "Are the teeny-weeny baby first years worried about their first test?"

Pearl frowned at him. She and her friends had met Mullet on the first day of school. At the start, he'd seemed nice. But he'd turned out to be a bully. He'd dared Flip to swim out into Bigsky Basin, and Flip had almost ended up being eaten by a shark out there!

"Oh, leave them alone, Mullet," Finny said.

"I don't blame them for being scared," Shelly added. "Bay's tests are really hard!"

"Really?" Pearl felt more worried than ever. Shelly might be Mullet's friend, but she was nothing like him. She seemed really cool. If she said something, it was probably true.

"Definitely!" Shelly widened her eyes. "I had to take my first Magic test three times before I passed!"

Mullet laughed. "That's because you kept cheating by singing to strengthen your magic," he said.

"Yeah," Finny agreed. "Bay kept telling you not to do that, since we hadn't studied it yet."

"I can't help it if I have natural talent." Shelly whistled a short tune. Then she turned back to Pearl and the others, looking sympathetic.

"Plus, I only sang because I had to. Good luck with the test."

Mullet sneered. "You're going to need it!"

4

Hard Work

PEARL HAD BEEN NERVOUS ABOUT THE MAGIC test before. But now she was really nervous.

Splash didn't seem to be nervous at all. He laughed, and said, "I'm not so sure about how I'll do. But Echo, I bet you'll do great. After all, you have your lucky shell to help you!"

"That's true." Pearl looked at Echo's necklace. "Too bad we don't all have lucky charms from your mom like that!"

"Oh, wow!" Shelly said. "Your mom has the strongest magic in all of the Salty Sea!"

Echo smiled confidently and rubbed Pearl's fin. "We're all going to do fine on the test. Don't worry, Pearl!"

At that moment, Riptide called for attention again. The ray was gone, and it was time to go back to class.

"Great!" Splash did two quick flips. "Time for Jumping and Swimming. Let's go!"

Pearl followed her friends out of the cove. Jumping and Swimming class always took place in the open water outside the coral, where there was more room to move around.

"Shake a fin, class!" Riptide bellowed as he zipped past them. "We're starting late because of that ray, and we have a lot of work to do today!"

He wasn't exaggerating. He started class by asking the students to show him everything they'd been practicing so far—swimming fast, doing flips in and out of the water, and more. Pearl was already tired by the time she finished all that.

Then Riptide called for attention again. "Now we're going to learn something special," he said with a big grin. "It's a trick I learned from a dolphin who lived with Land Leggers when he was younger."

"What do you mean?" Flip asked. "Land Leggers live on the land, and dolphins live in the water!"

"That's right," Riptide said. "Some Land Leggers caught this fellow and brought him to a special pool of water surrounded by land. They kept him there for a while before they brought him back home."

Echo shuddered. "That sounds horrible! I

wouldn't want to be stuck on a bunch of land."

Pearl nodded. She liked looking at the island where the baby turtles hatched. But she definitely wouldn't want to get any closer than the surf breaking on the beach.

"Never mind that." Riptide sounded impatient. "The Land Leggers taught him a fun trick, and he taught me. Now I'm going to teach you. It's called tail walking, and it goes something like this."

He led them to the surface. Pearl watched in amazement as Riptide lifted himself out of the water—and scooted backward while almost fully upright, with only his tail still in the water propelling him along!

"Wow!" Splash shouted when the teacher finally collapsed back into the water. "That was so cool!"

Most of the other students seemed to agree. Even Echo looked impressed.

But Pearl was worried. Tail walking looked really hard!

She turned out to be right. Tail walking was hard. It only took Splash a few tries to be able to do it, but even he couldn't stay upright for nearly as long as Riptide had. Flip, Harmony, and one of the other males started to get it after a few tries, too. Echo and the other two students weren't as good, but at least they could lift themselves all the way up and wiggle a little before flopping back down.

But not Pearl. No matter how hard she tried, she could only lift herself halfway out of the water. By the end of class, she was exhausted and discouraged.

"Never mind, Pearl." Echo touched her fin as the class swam slowly back toward the coral reef. "It's a hard trick. But I'm sure you'll get it."

"Yeah, I can help you practice later," Splash offered.

"Me too," Flip said. "I'm sure I'll be just as good as Riptide before long. Maybe even better!"

Pearl just nodded. She wasn't sure she'd ever be able to tail walk—no matter how much her friends tried to help!

Harmony swam past with a couple of the others. "I hope Riptide doesn't give us a test on tail walking anytime soon," she was saying.

Pearl gulped. "Do you think he will?" she asked her friends. "I'm definitely not ready for a test on tail walking—or anything else we're doing in Jumping and Swimming, either!"

"He hasn't said anything about a test," Flip said as they all swam in through the cove entrance. "We probably won't have one anytime soon."

"I hope not." Pearl blew out a sad stream of bubbles. "I'm just not very good at that class."

"Don't worry, Pearl." Splash swam a circle around her, then touched her fin. "Hey, if we do have a test, maybe Echo will lend you her lucky shell! That might help, right?"

"Sure." Echo smiled and lifted her fin as if to touch her necklace. Then she gasped. "Oh no! My lucky shell—it's gone!"

5

Missing Magic

"WHAT DO YOU MEAN, YOUR SHELL IS GONE?" Pearl swam closer to her. Sure enough, there was no sign of Echo's necklace! It was strange to see her not wearing it. "Oh no!" Echo cried again, spinning around in the water. "The seaweed string must have broken during class."

"Probably," Flip agreed. "You hit the water pretty hard while doing all that tail walking."

"I have to go back and find it!" Echo exclaimed.

"You can't," Splash said. "Ocean Lore starts in a few minutes. You'll get in trouble if you're late."

"I don't care." Echo sounded frantic. "I have to find my shell!"

Pearl was worried, too. Echo's lucky shell was really special. But she also didn't want her friend to get in trouble for skipping class.

"We'll help you find it right after school," she said. "We promise. Right, guys?"

"Right!" Splash said, and Flip nodded.

Echo hesitated, still staring out through the entrance toward the open water outside. But finally she nodded, too.

"Okay," she said. "I guess I can wait."

Ocean Lore seemed to pass even more slowly than usual. Old Salty spent the first half of the class talking about the feeding habits of tube worms. Then he switched to describing the different types of sea slugs in the area. Pearl was pretty sure she wouldn't remember anything the teacher was saying. She was too worried about Echo. What if they couldn't find her lucky shell?

Finally Old Salty dismissed them. Magic class was next. As Pearl and her friends swam past the school entrance, Echo paused.

"I wish I could go look for my shell now instead of waiting," she said. "What if the current carries it away?"

"The current isn't very strong where we were," Splash pointed out.

Pearl touched Echo's fin. "Come on. We only have one more class, and then we'll find your shell."

Echo nodded and followed Pearl and the

boys. But as soon as they reached the Magic area, she swam over to Bay.

"May I be excused for a few minutes?" Echo asked the teacher. "I lost my lucky shell during Jumping and Swimming, and I need to go out and find it."

"I'm sorry, Echo," Bay said. "You'll have to do that after class. The test is the day after tomorrow, and we have a lot of work to do before then."

"But I won't do as well without my lucky magic shell," Echo argued. "I won't be gone long."

"I said no, Echo." Bay's voice was kind but firm. "Now take your spot and let's get started."

Echo stared at the teacher for a moment without moving or saying anything. Finally she turned with a flip of her tail and swam over to Pearl.

"Can you believe she's being so mean?" Echo whispered. "I thought she'd understand!"

Pearl gave her a sympathetic look. But she didn't say anything, because Bay was already talking about the lesson plan for that day.

"We'll start by reviewing what we did yesterday," the teacher was saying. "Since some of you had trouble guiding the school of fish, we're going to back up to a smaller number of creatures." She waved a fin at three cute little striped coral shrimp clinging to a piece of mushroom coral on the seafloor. "I'd like each of you to guide those shrimp to climb down off the coral. Now, who wants to go first?"

Pearl expected Echo to volunteer, like

she usually did. But Echo was staring at the seafloor, looking distracted and anxious.

"I'll try!" Flip called out. "I'll probably do great without Splash holding me back." He glanced at Splash. "No offense."

Flip swam up for a breath of air. Then he returned and focused on the shrimp. It took him a long time, but he finally got two of them to hop down from the coral. The third one stayed where she was, but Bay still looked pleased.

"Well done, Flip," she said. "Who else would like to give it a try? Echo, how about you?"

"I guess," Echo muttered. While Bay guided the shrimp back onto the coral, Echo swam slowly up to the surface to take a breath and sank even more slowly back down.

"What's taking her so long?" Pearl heard Harmony whisper just behind her.

"Go ahead," Bay said. "Whenever you're ready, Echo."

Echo sent out a burst of magic energy. One of the shrimp moved a few steps toward the edge of the coral. But the other two stayed still.

Pearl held her breath, expecting Echo to try again. Instead, she felt the magic energy stop.

Echo backed away and looked at Bay.

"I can't do it," she said. "Not without my lucky shell."

"Nonsense," Bay said firmly. "Try again, please."

Echo frowned, looking as if she wanted to argue. Instead, she swam back over to the shrimp and sent out another weak burst of energy.

"Go, Echo!" Splash cheered. "You can do it!"

But the shrimp didn't budge. They just sat there, their long antennae waving in the current.

"Come on, Echo," Bay said. "I know you can do better than that."

"No, I can't!" Echo sent out a sudden wild burst of magic energy. The shrimp all jumped up as if an electric ray had just shocked them, then leaped off the coral. One scuttled off across the seafloor, while the others hid under the coral's wavy edge.

Bay frowned. "I asked you to guide them, not push them."

Pearl's eyes widened in surprise. Pushing was related to guiding, but more advanced—and much less nice. While guiding was a way of asking creatures to do something, pushing was a way of forcing them. Dolphins weren't supposed to push other creatures unless it was absolutely necessary.

"I didn't mean to!" Echo's muzzle quivered, and her fins flapped in distress. "It's hard to control my magic without my shell to help."

Bay didn't say anything for a moment. Finally she blew out a narrow stream of bubbles.

"All right, let me gather the shrimp again,"

she said. "Harmony, you can go next."

Pearl reached for Echo's fin when she swam back over. But Echo kept her fins close to her body, out of reach.

Pearl wasn't sure what to think about how her friend was acting. She was used to Echo being the most talented in the class at magic. Could it really just have been her lucky shell all along?

6

The Search Is On

As soon as Bay dismissed the class, Echo flicked her tail and zipped away in a stream of bubbles. "Hurry!" she called back.

Pearl, Splash, and Flip swam after her. They caught up at the school entrance, and all four of them swam out together. They'd left class so fast that no other students had left yet.

"Slow down, Echo," Flip said breathlessly. "Pearl is probably getting tired from trying to keep up with you." Then he swam up to get some air.

Pearl went with him. While both their heads were above the surface, she said, "Do you think we can find her shell? It's pretty small."

"I'm sure I can find it," Flip said. "I'm good at stuff like that."

He dove down, and Pearl followed. She hoped Flip was right!

The Jumping and Swimming class area was deeper than the rest of the school, but not too deep for sunlight to reach the seafloor. There weren't any large coral formations, but there were plenty of smaller bits of rock and coral, along with patches of seaweed and lots of shells.

"It's going to be hard to spot it here," Splash said. "It could have fallen anywhere!"

"We have to find it!" Echo snapped, glaring at him.

"It's okay," Pearl said quickly. "We will."

She swam lower, pushing aside a clump of seaweed with her snout to check for the shell. But it wasn't there, so she moved on to a small pile of shells and started sifting through them with her muzzle and fins.

"Hey, what are you babies doing down there?" a familiar voice called.

It was Mullet. When Pearl looked up, he was floating above them near the surface. Finny and Shelly were nowhere in sight.

"We're searching for Echo's lucky shell," Splash told the older dolphin. "She lost it during class today."

"You lost your lucky charm, Echo?" Mullet said mockingly. "Uh-oh, now you'll never pass your Magic test!"

Echo stopped searching and swam up to him. "What are you doing here, Mullet?" she demanded. "Did you steal my lucky shell?"

"What? No!" Now Mullet sounded annoyed. "Why would I want to take your dumb baby toy?"

"I bet you did!" Echo swam even closer, glaring into his face. "You were hanging around us during recess—I bet you grabbed it then!"

Pearl traded a worried look with Splash. "I don't think so," Splash said. "We would have noticed if he did that."

"Not if he was sneaky about it," Echo said. "And we all know Mullet's totally sneaky!"

Mullet just glared at Echo. Then he swam away without another word.

Uh-oh, Pearl thought. *He seemed kind of insulted. I hope this doesn't make him even meaner to us!*

But she didn't say anything out loud. Echo was staring after Mullet. She didn't look angry anymore, though. Now she looked sad.

"How am I going to tell my mom I lost her special gift?" she said. "She picked it out just for me."

"I know." Pearl swam over and rubbed her fin. "Don't worry—you might not have to tell her. We still have time to find it."

"Yeah," Splash said. "We hardly started looking yet!"

"Anyway, your mom probably won't be that upset," Flip said. "It's just a shell. There are lots of them in the sea."

"What?" Echo squeaked, a wild stream of bubbles escaping from her blowhole. "How can you say that?"

"Because it's true!" Flip said. "Your mom

probably won't even notice the necklace is missing."

"Of course she will!" Echo exclaimed. "That shell is special! You know that. It has some of Mom's magic in it. That's why I was having so much trouble in class today." She glared at him. "Wait a second—you didn't take it, did you?"

"Huh?" Pearl said. "Why would he do that?"

"Because he's jealous of my mom's magic and mine, too." Echo frowned. "That's probably why he's always talking about it. I bet he saw my shell fall off today during class and hid it somewhere!"

"Are you kidding? I wouldn't do that!" Flip cried. "I can't believe you would think that. You should apologize to me!"

"You should give back my shell!" Echo yelled in return.

Flip puffed out a whole cloud of bubbles. Then he spun around and swam away as fast as he could.

7

Echo in Trouble

THE NEXT MORNING, ECHO WAS WAITING BY
the entrance when Pearl arrived at school.
"I'm glad you're here," Echo said. "I need to
tell you something."

"What is it?" Pearl asked. She could tell that
Echo was still upset. Even though Pearl, Echo,
and Splash had searched until it was almost
dark, they hadn't found Echo's necklace.

Echo blew out a few bubbles. "I didn't want
to tell my mom I lost my lucky shell," she said.
"So I told her I loaned it to you—you know, to

help you study for that Magic test tomorrow."

"You did?" Pearl felt uneasy. It wasn't like Echo to lie—especially to her mother. Losing her lucky charm wasn't just making Echo worse at magic. It seemed to be turning her into an entirely different type of dolphin!

Pearl wanted to say that to Echo, but she didn't dare. They hadn't been friends for very long. Pearl didn't want Echo to get mad at her like she had at Flip yesterday. She definitely didn't want Echo to accuse her of stealing the lucky shell!

"I wanted to tell you, just in case you see my mom," Echo said. "You know, so you don't give away what really happened."

That made Pearl feel even worse. She didn't want to lie to Echo's mother—or anyone else, for that matter! But she figured she probably wouldn't see Echo's mother, anyway. So she just nodded.

"Come on," she said. "We should get to class."

Echo was quiet during Music class. When it was her turn to sing, Pearl could barely hear her. Pearl also noticed that Echo and Flip were staying as far apart as they could. She was pretty sure that Bay noticed, too. But the teacher didn't say anything about that, or about Echo's weak singing, either.

When it was time to go to Jumping and Swimming, Flip swam off ahead by himself, even though Splash called out for him to wait. "Are you and Flip still mad at each other?" Pearl asked Echo.

Echo shrugged. "I guess so," she said. "I don't know. I barely saw him after school yesterday, and he left without me this morning.

I swam here with some of the older kids from my pod."

Soon they arrived at Jumping and Swimming class. Riptide announced that they wouldn't be practicing tail walking that day.

"Some of you had more trouble than I expected," he said. "We're going to do swim sprints today instead. That will make your tails stronger for when we return to tail walking."

Pearl almost groaned. Swim sprints were hard! But they weren't as hard as tail walking, so she didn't complain.

Riptide told the whole class to line up behind a cluster of oysters. When he gave the word, the dolphins were supposed to swim as fast as they could to the edge of a seaweed bed, then flip in the water and swim back just as fast.

"First one back gets to rest during the next round!" Riptide shouted. "Go!"

Pearl whipped her tail back and forth as hard as she could to propel herself forward. She wished Riptide had given them a chance to take a breath first, since she didn't have much air left. But she did her best, anyway, swimming as fast as she could.

As she reached the seaweed, she focused on her flip. She'd been the worst one in the class at flipping on the first day. But she'd been practicing at home, with Squeak helping her. Splash had been helping her whenever he could, too. And all that practice paid off! Pearl flipped smoothly without getting disoriented, slowing down, or bumping into anyone else. She was so excited that she zipped forward even faster on the way back.

When she stopped after the oyster bed, she looked around. Splash, Flip, Harmony, and one of the others were already there. But the rest of the class was behind her!

"Awesome job, Pearl!" Splash exclaimed, touching her fin. "You came in fifth!"

"Yeah, you're definitely getting faster," Flip said. "Not as fast as me, but faster!"

Pearl smiled. "Thanks," she said with a little burst of bubbles.

She looked for Echo, expecting her to congratulate her, too. But Echo wasn't back yet. She was floating halfway across the course, swimming slowly along near the seafloor well behind the others.

Riptide noticed, too. "Echo!" he bellowed. "Shake a fin! This is a sprint, not a dawdle!"

"I bet she's trying to look for her shell," Splash whispered.

Pearl thought he was right. But she didn't think it was a good idea to do it during class. Riptide was pretty strict.

Echo sped up and crossed the finish line. But after that, each time the class did a sprint, Echo came in last. After Riptide noticed her dawdling for the third time, he lost his patience.

"That's enough!" he barked. "If you're not

8

Pearl's Plan

As soon as Echo finished her laps, Pearl and Splash swam over to her. Riptide was already swimming off toward the cove.

"We thought we could search again for a while, if you want," Splash told Echo.

"Really?" Echo brightened. "Thanks, guys. You're good friends." She rubbed Pearl's fin, then Splash's.

Pearl smiled. But she couldn't stop herself from thinking, *I want you to find your shell so you'll become a good friend again, too!*

She immediately felt guilty. Her father had a favorite saying: *Always choose kindness.* Pearl had a feeling he wouldn't think she was being very kind in her thoughts right now.

So she did her best to push those thoughts out of her mind as she started searching. Splash was already nosing through some tangled seaweed.

"I'm pretty sure I checked that bed yesterday," Pearl told him.

"Okay," Splash said. "I'll look over by those rocks."

Pearl glanced around. The Jumping and Swimming area was so big! It was hard to keep track of where everyone had looked already. How were they ever going to find one tiny shell in all this space?

Then she noticed a sea turtle swimming by.

That gave her an idea.

"Hey, I know what we could try," she told Echo and Splash. "There are lots of creatures who live around here all the time. We could try asking them if they've seen your shell!"

"You mean messaging them?" Splash asked.

"Uh-huh," Pearl said.

Mental messaging was one of the simplest types of magic. It was a way for dolphins to talk to one another at a distance. It could also be used to communicate with other species. Dolphins were the only sea creatures who understood words and complicated ideas, but other animals could understand simple pictures and emotions. Most of the new students had only started learning about sending mental messages to other species at the beginning of the school year, but Pearl had been practicing on the sea turtles in her lagoon for a long time.

"Great idea, Pearl!" Splash did an excited flip. "Let's try it!"

"You guys go ahead," Echo said. "I'd better just keep searching the regular way. I don't have much control over my magic right now, remember?"

Pearl traded a worried look with Splash. "Okay," she said. "We'll give it a try."

She spotted a spiny lobster and swam over. Focusing on him, Pearl formed a picture of Echo's lucky shell in her mind. She sent out a beam of magic, aiming it at the lobster.

He stayed still for a moment. Then Pearl received a weak picture of lots of shells. A moment later, the lobster scuttled away.

"Oops, I guess he didn't understand me,"

Pearl said. "I'll try again."

This time she sent a message to a pretty blue parrot fish. She was careful to make the picture in her mind as clear as she could. The parrot fish seemed to understand. She darted down and nosed at a shell on the seafloor.

"No, that's not the one," Pearl said. "It looks like this . . ." She tried again. But the parrot fish seemed to be bored of the game. With a flick of her tail, she disappeared into a hole in some coral.

But Pearl kept trying. So did Splash, even though he wasn't that good at mental messaging. They sent their message to fish, some shrimp, a sea cucumber, and every other creature they could find.

Finally Pearl approached a large grouper. She sent him the picture of the missing shell.

The grouper hung in the water not moving, and for a moment, Pearl thought he was ignoring her. She was about to move on when she got a blurry image back from the grouper—showing Echo's shell lying on the sand!

"That's it!" she cried, even though she knew the grouper couldn't understand her words. "Will you show us?"

She sent an image of the grouper leading her and the other dolphins to the shell. Splash swam over and added his magic to hers to make the message stronger.

Once again, the grouper stayed still for a long moment. Then he turned and swam slowly away, leading them past the oyster bed and around a clump of brain coral. Pearl and Splash called Echo to follow them.

"Where's he taking us?" Splash wondered.

Echo blew out a stream of bubbles. "I don't think he understands," she said. "We weren't even over this far yesterday! Let's go back."

"No, wait," Pearl said. "Let's see where he's going."

A short distance later, the grouper dove down toward the seafloor. Pearl followed—and gasped.

"That's it!" she said. "Echo, I think it's your lucky shell!"

Echo darted forward to look. "It is!" she cried happily. "Oh, thank you!"

As the grouper swam off, a bright orange claw poked out of the shell. Then another. Pearl's eyes widened.

"Is that a hermit crab?" she said.

A pair of eyestalks poked out next. "Hey,

Echo, it looks like he's moved into your shell!"
Splash said, giggling.

"It's not funny. He has to get out!" Echo
exclaimed. She nosed at the shell, but that
didn't do anything.

"Watch out for his claws!" Pearl warned.

Echo backed away and sent out a burst of
magic energy toward the hermit crab. Pearl
caught part of the image Echo was sending—
it showed the crab scuttling quickly out of her
lucky shell.

The hermit crab shrank back into the shell. The message he sent back wasn't really an image at all. It was more of a feeling. And that feeling was: *NO!*

Echo frowned. "He has to get out," she insisted. "Join your magic with mine, okay? I'm going to push him."

"Don't do that!" Pearl exclaimed.

"I'm going to," Echo insisted. "Are you going to help me or not?"

Pearl hesitated. She didn't want Echo to get mad at her. But she couldn't do something she knew was wrong, either.

"I'm not," she said at last. "It's not right. We're supposed to be the protectors of the ocean, remember? There has to be another way."

Echo frowned. She looked at the hermit crab, and then at Pearl. Finally she sighed.

"I guess you're right," she said. "My mom wouldn't want me to push him, either—not even to get my lucky shell back. But how am I going to get him out of there?"

Splash was looking toward the cove. "Hey, it's time for Ocean Lore," he said. "We should get back."

Echo stared at her shell, looking anxious. Pearl touched her fin.

"It's okay," she said. "Hermit crabs can't travel very fast. Your shell will still be here after school. We'll figure out what to do then."

9

The Hermit Crab

PEARL COULD TELL THAT ECHO WAS EXTRA distracted and missing her shell during Magic class. She messed up every exercise she tried. She couldn't even guide an angelfish to turn around without accidentally sending it crashing into some coral!

"She's worse than ever," Splash whispered as Echo darted up to take a breath before trying again. "I thought she'd be better now that she knows where her shell is."

"Maybe it's true that most of her magic

comes from her lucky charm," Pearl whispered back.

"Hmm." Splash seemed dubious, but he shrugged. "In that case, we'd better figure out how to get her shell back fast. The test is tomorrow!"

Pearl nodded. A couple of days ago, she would have loved to have a lucky shell like Echo's to help her with that test. But now she was starting to think it was more trouble than it was worth!

After school, Echo rushed off toward the exit again. "Wait up!" Pearl called.

"Hurry," Echo said, barely slowing down. "I don't want that hermit crab to wander off with my shell."

Pearl sneaked a look at Flip. She was pretty sure he was close enough to hear them. But he wasn't looking their way. He was listening to the other two boys in their school pod talk about tomorrow's test.

Soon Pearl, Echo, and Splash were gathered around the hermit crab. He'd barely moved from the spot where they'd found him.

"Please," Echo said. "I need my shell back!" She sent the crab a message and put her fin on the shell. But he didn't even send a message back.

"Hermit crabs need a shell to be safe, right?" Pearl said. "It's his home. But maybe if we offer him a different shell, he'll switch."

"Great idea!" Splash said. "We can probably find one he'll like even better."

The three of them swam around looking for shells. Pearl found several around the right size. They were all different colors and patterns.

"Look at this one," Echo said, dropping a shell beside the hermit crab. "It's really pretty, isn't it?"

"Definitely!" Pearl agreed. The shell Echo had found had swirls and stripes of bright color. It was almost exactly the same size and shape as her lucky shell.

Splash did a flip. "Let's tell him to come out and look. I bet he'll love it!"

They touched fins and sent a mental message to the hermit crab. But he didn't even poke his eyestalks out.

"Let's try guiding him to look out," Pearl said. She glanced at Echo. "But no pushing!"

"I promise I won't." Once again, the three friends joined their magic. Soon the hermit crab was peeking out with his long eyestalks, swiveling them toward the pile of shells.

"Now we'll send him a message showing him that he should switch," Pearl urged.

Echo nodded and they all sent out a wave of magic. But the crab only stared at them suspiciously, then pulled himself back into Echo's shell. The mental message he sent back was weak and not very clear, but Pearl could guess what it meant: He thought this shell was perfect. He wasn't going to budge!

"Ugh!" Echo cried. "Why is he being so stubborn?"

Before Pearl could answer, she heard voices

nearby. Splash heard them, too.

"Uh-oh," he whispered. "Mullet and Shelly are coming this way!"

"Oh no," Pearl murmured. The last thing they needed right now was for Mullet to start teasing them—or worse, for him to scare the hermit crab away while he was still in Echo's shell!

Echo looked determined. "I don't think they saw us yet," she whispered. "I have an idea . . ."

Pearl felt magic energy pouring out of her friend. She wasn't sure what Echo was doing, and for a moment, she hesitated. Was Echo going to try something she shouldn't—like pushing the crab?

Suddenly a large school of mackerel zipped into view. There were so many of them that they formed a shiny silver curtain in the water, totally blocking Mullet and Shelly from view.

By the time the fish zipped away again, Mullet and Shelly were gone. They'd swum right by on the other side of the mackerel without seeing Pearl and the others!

"Wow!" Splash said. "Good thinking, Echo."

Pearl stared at Echo. "Did you guide those fish over here?" she asked.

"Yes," Echo said. "I saw them a few minutes ago when I was looking for shells. I'm glad they were still close enough for me to get them."

Pearl nodded thoughtfully. Guiding that many fish at once wasn't easy for any dolphin—especially one their age. But Echo had performed the difficult magic perfectly, even though she still didn't have her shell back!

"Echo, that's hard to do! This means you don't need your lucky shell to do magic!" Pearl exclaimed.

But Echo wouldn't listen. "It was just luck," she insisted.

Pearl was frustrated. But suddenly she had an idea—she was pretty sure there was one dolphin who could help her convince Echo of the truth . . .

10

The Test

Pearl swam closer and touched Echo's fin again. "I don't think we can convince the hermit crab to leave on our own," she said. "We need help. I think we should tell your mom what happened."

"What?" Echo looked alarmed. "But then she'll know I lost my lucky shell!"

"But she'll also know you found it again," Pearl said. "And maybe she can help you figure out what to do."

Echo sank down toward the seafloor,

looking uncertain. "I guess you're right," she said. "But let's hurry. I really need my shell back before tomorrow!"

Pearl, Echo, and Splash swam as fast as they could to Echo's pod. "Wish me luck!" Echo whispered as they spotted her mother.

"Don't worry," Pearl said. "We'll be right beside you."

"Yeah," Splash agreed.

Echo led the way over to her mother.

"Pearl! Splash!" Echo's mother said. "It's nice to see you again. Did you come to do more studying?"

"Not exactly," Echo answered for them. "Mom, something terrible happened . . ." She told her the whole story.

Her mother listened quietly without saying anything. "I see," she said when Echo finished.

"So you have to help me convince that crab to give back my shell right away!" Echo said. "The Magic test is tomorrow, and without the magic in my shell to help, I'll probably fail!"

"Oh, Echo." Her mother blew out a stream of bubbles. "Is that really what you believe?"

"Of course!" Echo said. "Some of your magic is in that shell. That's why I do so well at magic." She flapped a fin. "Or at least why I used to. Ever since I lost the shell, I can barely guide a fish to swim!"

Her mother shook her head. "But, Echo, there's no magic in that shell," she said kindly. "I just thought it was pretty, and that's why I gave it to you."

Echo looked surprised. But Pearl wasn't surprised at all. She'd guessed that Echo's mother would say that—and that Echo might even listen.

"No magic?" Echo said. "Then why have I been messing up in class the past two days?"

Flip swam over just in time to hear her. "Yeah," he said sullenly. "And why has she been acting like such an algae-head since then, too?"

"What do you mean?" Echo demanded. "I haven't been acting any different—well, except for being worried about my lucky shell."

"Yes you have," Pearl blurted out. "You haven't been acting like yourself at all."

"Yeah," Splash agreed. "The regular Echo wouldn't ever think Flip stole her shell."

"Oh." Echo looked sheepish. "Um, maybe you're right. I'm sorry, Flip. I know you wouldn't do that."

"Thank you!" Flip looked happier.

Echo turned to her mother. "And I'm really sorry for losing your special gift," she said. "Even if it isn't magic, I still love it. And I still want it back."

"I know." Her mother rubbed her fin. "But you can't force the hermit crab to move out. It wouldn't be right."

Pearl had just been thinking the same thing. "I'm pretty sure that hermit crab loves your shell just as much as you do," she told Echo. "And he needs it more than you do—after all, it's his whole world!"

"Wow," Echo said. "I never thought about it that way." She looked troubled. "I know dolphins are supposed to help other creatures. But it's not fair—that shell is my lucky charm."

"The only lucky charm you need is yourself, your friends, and your pod," her mother told her.

"Okay," Echo said. "I guess you're right."

But Pearl could tell her friend still wasn't quite sure. "Come on," she said to distract Echo. "As long as we're all here, let's go practice for that test, okay?"

The next day was the test. "It's going to be simple, since this is your first test," Bay said. "See that butterfly fish? I want each of you to guide her to swim in a circle, then circle back the other way. Pearl? Why don't you start us off?"

Pearl gulped, suddenly more nervous than ever. She swam up and took a breath. Then she focused on the butterfly fish.

For a moment, nothing happened. The fish just stared back at her, her bright yellow fins waving in the current.

Oh no! Pearl thought. *What if I can't do this?*

She glanced at her friends. They were all smiling at her. She smiled back and tried again, imagining that all their magic was mingling with hers.

And this time it worked! The butterfly fish swam forward, curving into a circle. Pearl carefully guided her all the way around, then back the other way.

"Well done, Pearl!" Bay said. "You've passed. I'm proud of you. Harmony? Why don't you go next . . ."

Pearl was relieved that she'd passed the test. But when she looked at Echo, she still felt nervous. Did Echo really believe she could do magic without that shell, or would she mess up again like she had for the past two days?

When it was finally Echo's turn, Pearl saw

her touch her fin to the spot where her lucky charm used to be. For a second, Echo looked nervous.

"It's okay," Pearl whispered to her. "You can do it!"

Echo rubbed her fin. "Thanks!" she whispered back. Then she swam forward—and guided the butterfly fish in two big, smooth circles.

"Yay, Echo!" Flip cheered, and Splash did three flips in a row to celebrate.

"We knew you could do it!" Pearl told her friend proudly.

"I wasn't totally sure I could," Echo said with a smile. "But it helped to know you all believed in me!"

Pearl smiled back. "I know exactly what you mean."

After school, Pearl and Echo swam out to see the hermit crab. "Do you want to try again to make him leave?" Pearl asked. "Maybe if we asked again nicely or found another really good shell . . ."

Echo didn't answer for a second. Swimming closer, she touched the shell with the tip of her muzzle.

Then she backed away. "No, it's all right," she said. "I don't need it, and he does. I'm glad he's happy."

Pearl rubbed her fin. "Me, too," she said. "Come on—let's go find Splash and Flip. We need to celebrate passing our very first test in dolphin school!"

Read on for a sneak

peek at the next

Dolphin
School

story!

Splash's Secret Friend

WHEN SCHOOL ENDED FOR THE DAY, Splash dashed out of the cove at top speed. "Hey, wait up!" Flip yelled, swimming after him.

Pearl and Echo followed. "Splash is still acting weird," Echo said as they swam. "What do you think is wrong?"

"I don't know," Pearl said. "But I hope he'll tell us. Maybe then we can help him."

They caught up to the boys outside. "What's the matter with you, anyway?" Flip was saying, sounding annoyed. "You're acting like a real barnacle-head today!"

"No, I'm not," Splash said. "I'm just in a

hurry to get home, that's all."

"You mean because of the shark migration?" Echo asked. "I don't blame you for being worried about that."

"Yeah." Pearl shivered. "I'm glad the migration will be over soon!"

"It doesn't have anything to do with sharks," Splash said. "I already told you that."

"A-ha!" Flip said. "You just admitted there's something wrong."

"No I didn't," Splash said. "There's nothing wrong."

"Then why did you say 'It doesn't have anything to do with sharks'?" Flip said. "That's admitting there's something wrong—just not sharks, right?"

Splash's fins drooped. "Okay, you caught

me." He blew bubbles out of his blowhole in a big sigh. "Anyway, I hate trying to keep a secret from my best friends."

"A secret?" Echo said. "What kind of secret?"

Splash looked around, then swam closer and lowered his voice. "If I tell you, do you promise you won't be upset?"

Pearl looked at the others. What kind of secret would upset them? Wondering made her feel a little nervous.

"We promise," Echo said after a moment. "Right, guys?"

"Sure, I promise," Pearl said.

"Me, too," Flip added. "Now what's your big secret, Splash?"

"I'll show you," Splash said. "But you have to promise one more thing. You can't tell anyone else, no matter what. Nobody. I mean it."

"Okay," Flip said right away.

But this time Echo hesitated even longer, looking uneasy. Pearl knew how she felt, since she didn't really like the thought of making that kind of promise. She was used to telling her parents everything. She didn't want to keep any secrets from her teachers, either.

"Do you promise?" Splash asked the two girls.

Finally Echo nodded. "I promise," she said in a quiet voice.

"I do, too," Pearl said. Splash was their friend. She knew he wouldn't ask them to keep a secret unless it was something really important.

"Good." Splash sounded a little happier. "Then come with me."

He swam off away from the school reef. His friends followed.

"We're not going to Bigsky Basin, are we?" Flip asked.

He sounded nervous, and Pearl could guess why. On the first day of school, Mullet had dared Flip to swim out into the deeper water of the Basin all by himself. He'd run into a huge tiger shark out there, and had barely escaped. Pearl still felt scared when she thought about it. She wondered if any sharks were migrating through Bigsky Basin right at that moment. Either way, she was glad when Splash said they weren't going anywhere near there.

"So where are we going?" Echo asked,

flicking her fluke to catch up with Splash.

"You'll see." Splash glanced behind him. "Nobody saw us swim this way, did they?"

"I don't think so," Pearl said. "But aren't you going to tell us where you're taking us?"

"To meet a new friend," Splash said.

"A new friend?" Flip said. "What do you mean? Another dolphin?"

"No," Splash said. "Please don't ask any more questions, okay? You should wait and see for yourselves."

"Okay," Pearl said. She tried to imagine what kind of friend Splash meant. If it wasn't a dolphin, it had to be some other kind of sea creature. But why would Splash think they'd be upset if he'd made friends with a lobster or a manta ray or something?

Pearl had befriended several of the sea turtles who lived in her home lagoon. Her little sister, Squeak, was good friends with a reef squid who lived there, too.

Splash was swimming even faster now, so Pearl had to work hard to keep up. When they neared a large clump of stony coral, he stopped suddenly.

"We're almost there," he said, sounding nervous. "Don't forget your promise, okay?"

"We won't," Echo said. "Now where's this new friend of yours?"

"Is that him over there?" Flip swam toward a passing puffer fish. But the fish ignored him and kept swimming. "Oh. I guess not."

Pearl looked around. There weren't

many fish or other sea creatures nearby. The only ones she saw were an eel and a couple of sea urchins. Was one of those creatures Splash's new friend?

"Okay." Splash blew out a stream of bubbles. "Are you guys ready to meet him now?"

"Hold on, I'm almost out of air," Echo said. She swam up to the surface and sucked in a breath. Pearl and Flip did the same.

So did Splash. Only instead of stopping right at the surface, he kept going. He burst out of the water and did an unusual spinning leap.

When he splashed back down again, Flip looked impressed. "Hey, where'd you learn to do that jump?" he exclaimed. "You've got to teach me—I bet even Riptide would be impressed if we showed him that move!"

"Just come on," Splash said without answering him. "It's this way."

He darted off, swimming around the coral. The others followed. Once again, Pearl had to swim as fast as she could to keep up.

But when she rounded the coral, she stopped short. Splash was just ahead— snout to snout with a shark!

The Rescue Princesses

These are no ordinary princesses—
they're Rescue Princesses!

Puppy Powers

Get your paws on the Puppy Powers series!

There's something special about the animals at Power's Pets . . . something downright magical!

Secret Kingdom

Be in on the secret.
Collect them all!

Enjoy six sparkling adventures.

Secret Kingdom: Enchanted Palace
ROSIE BANKS

Secret Kingdom: Unicorn Valley
ROSIE BANKS

Secret Kingdom: Cloud Island
ROSIE BANKS

Secret Kingdom: Mermaid Reef
ROSIE BANKS

Secret Kingdom: Magic Mountain
ROSIE BANKS

Secret Kingdom: Glitter Beach
ROSIE BANKS

RAINBOW magic™

Which Magical Fairies Have You Met?

- ❑ The Rainbow Fairies
- ❑ The Weather Fairies
- ❑ The Jewel Fairies
- ❑ The Pet Fairies
- ❑ The Dance Fairies
- ❑ The Music Fairies
- ❑ The Sports Fairies
- ❑ The Party Fairies
- ❑ The Ocean Fairies
- ❑ The Night Fairies
- ❑ The Magical Animal Fairies
- ❑ The Princess Fairies
- ❑ The Superstar Fairies
- ❑ The Fashion Fairies
- ❑ The Sugar & Spice Fairies
- ❑ The Earth Fairies
- ❑ The Magical Crafts Fairies

■ SCHOLASTIC

SCHOLASTIC and associated logos are trademarks and/or registered trademarks of Scholastic Inc. © 2015 Rainbow Magic Limited. HIT and the HIT Entertainment logo are trademarks of HIT Entertainment Limited.

Find all of your favorite fairy friends at
scholastic.com/rainbowmagic

HiT entertainment

RMFAIRY11